LONE WOLF and CUB

by
KAZUO KOIKE
and
GOSEKI KOJIMA

cover by
FRANK MILLER
and
LYNN VARLEY

第3巻

小島剛夕 小池一夫

子連れ狼

FIRST PUBLISHING

Kazuo Koike
STORY

Goseki Kojima
ART

Frank Miller
COVER ILLUSTRATION & INTRODUCTION

David Lewis, Christine Miyuki Martine, Alex Wald
ENGLISH ADAPTATION

Willie Schubert
LETTERING

Paul Guinan
PRODUCTION

Rick Oliver
EDITOR

Rick Obadiah
PUBLISHER

Alex Wald
ART DIRECTOR

Kathy Kotsivas
OPERATIONS DIRECTOR

Rick Taylor
PRODUCTION MANAGER

Kurt Goldzung
SALES DIRECTOR

Lone Wolf and Cub (Kozure Okami) © 1987 Kazuo
Koike and Goseki Kojima.

English translation © 1987 First Comics, Inc. and Global
Communications Corporation.

Cover illustration and introduction © 1987 Frank Miller.

Published monthly in the United States of America by First
Comics, Inc., 435 N. LaSalle, Chicago Il 60610, and Studio
Ship, Inc. under exclusive license by Global Communications
Corporation, Musashiya Building, 4th Floor, 27-10, Aobadai
1-Chome, Meguro-Ku, Tokyo, 153 Japan, owner of world wide
publishing rights to the property Lone Wolf and Cub.

Lone Wolf and Cub #3 (ISBN 0-915419-12-2) © 1987 First
Comics, Inc. and Global Communications Corporation. All
rights reserved.

First printing, July 1987.

The Japanese call comic books "manga," which, literally translated, means "irresponsible pictures." Some of their more serious cartoonists prefer to call them "gekiga," or "dramatic pictures," but, to most Japanese comic readers, manga are manga and accepted as a worthy and important part of their popular culture. They sell millions of copies to Japanese of all ages and both sexes, and offer an astonishing diversity in subject matter. Strolling through a manga shop, you'll see adventure comics of every conceivable type, romance comics, comics of historical fiction and historical fact, sports comics for lovers of baseball, kendo, and even fishing. [*editor's note: Kazuo Koike is currently working on a comic strip about his favorite sports passion — golf*] Riding any train in Japan, you'll see manga in the hands of schoolgirls and businessmen alike.

Kazuo Koike's and Goseki Kojima's *Lone Wolf and Cub* first began appearing in 1970, and has enjoyed immense success not only as a comic book, but in faithful adaptations to television and film. Its story of a great samurai warrior and his quest for vengeance strikes a deep cord in Japanese history and culture. Like any really good novel, *Lone Wolf and Cub* is rich in themes that are as universal as they are human. Exotic as it may at first seem to western eyes, its thrilling action sequences and powerful emotional context make *Lone Wolf* great reading even for those to whom the Japanese are an alien, bewildering people.

Lone Wolf was not created in America, and wasn't fed through the meatgrinder of pressure groups and rating systems that we use to circumvent the First Amendment and its purpose of protecting freedom of expression. First Publishing is committed to running it uncensored, so it's bound to offend a number of those who think creative work should propagandize for their own political and religious beliefs. This segment, in particular, has as its focal point the premeditated murder of a priest. Since the priest is Buddhist, not Christian, it's not likely to draw fire from our right-wing evangelists, but pro-censorship liberals are sure to find it morally and politically incorrect, just as they are certainly not going to read it deeply enough or carefully enough to understand its profoundly Buddhist philosophical underpinnings.

Luckily for all of us, *Lone Wolf* is seeing print. You can read and judge it for yourself. I think you'll find that it's a terrific piece of work.

Frank Miller
Los Angeles, 1987

 **W**rongfully accused of plotting to overthrow the Shogun, **Itto Ogami** becomes an outlaw, wandering through the provinces of feudal Japan with his infant son **Daigoro** by his side, seeking vengeance for the murder of his wife and family.

Ogami survives by his wits — and frequently by offering his services as a paid assassin. Sometimes his victims deserve the death he coldly metes out; other times they do not. But either way, Ogami is utterly committed to his task if he accepts payment and gives his word of honor. That is the way of the Samurai.

Once Ogami had been the Shogun's official executioner, using his deft swordsmanship to end the lives of rebellious lords who defied the Shogun. His skills with the blade were legendary.

The Lone Wolf has chosen the assassin's road; but can he truly transcend himself and become the perfect assassin? Is it possible for him to reach the state of "Mu" — to feel nothing? "When you meet the Buddha, kill the Buddha." These words echo in Itto Ogami's mind when he is hired to kill a wise and benevolent priest who shows him the road to "The Gateless Barrier."

序
文

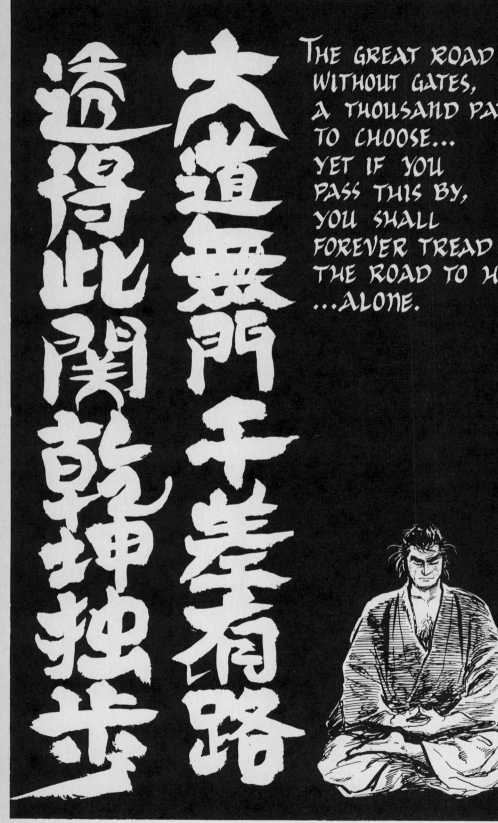

THE GREAT ROAD WITHOUT GATES, A THOUSAND PATHS TO CHOOSE... YET IF YOU PASS THIS BY, YOU SHALL FOREVER TREAD THE ROAD TO HELL ...ALONE.

大道無門千差有路透得此関乾坤独歩

THE GATELESS BARRIER

無門関

其之四

3

4

GRRR-- RAWR!

CHOMP!

GRRRR!

GNAW! SLURP!

SLOBBER

WHINE

IS IT POSSIBLE TO BECOME *ONE* WITH *MU*, NOTHINGNESS? TO *FORGET* THE SELF, WHERE SUBJECT AND OBJECT ARE AS ONE? TO BECOME A LEAF OF *NAIGEDAJO*-- TO FEEL *NOTHING* IS TO HAVE NO *BARRIERS*, NO *TIES* TO THE MATERIAL WORLD.

"WHEN YOU MEET THE *BUDDHA*, KILL THE *BUDDHA*. WHEN YOU MEET YOUR *PARENTS*, KILL YOUR *PARENTS*." IS IT POSSIBLE TO ACCEPT *NOTHING* IN THE WORLD, YET BE AT *ONE* WITH THE *UNIVERSE*?

UNTIL I *ACHIEVE* THAT STATE OF MIND I WILL NOT TAKE UP THIS *SWORD* AGAIN.

DEATH MOVES ON THE *WIND*, AND I AM BUT A *LEAF*.

MY BODY MAY TREAD THE SIX PATHS-- HEAVEN, HUMAN, MURDER, BEAST, DEMON, HELL...

THRUNSHO YAIIGH!

OR IT MAY PASS THROUGH THE FOUR LIVES-- THE SPAWN, THE EGG, THE WOMB, AND REINCARNATION... BUT TO *UNITE* THE *OPPOSITES* IN *MU*...

IT'S *IMPOSSIBLE*...

YOU'LL *NEVER* MAKE IT...

NEVER...

NEVER...

YOUR SON IS PRECIOUS. WHY MUST YOU TAKE HIM TO ŌGAMI-YAMA?

PUFF PUFF

ŌGAMI-YAMA IS ALSO KNOWN AS *WOLF* MOUNTAIN* BECAUSE OF THE PACKS THAT ROAM THERE. TO MAKE THINGS *WORSE*, THERE IS NO *FOOD* FOR THEM TO *HUNT* NOW. YOU'LL NEVER MAKE IT!

IMPOSSIBLE... NEVER... NEVER...

*ŌGAMI (GREAT GOD) AND ŌKAMI (WOLF) SOUND ALIKE AND ARE USED HERE FOR IRONIC INTENT.

8

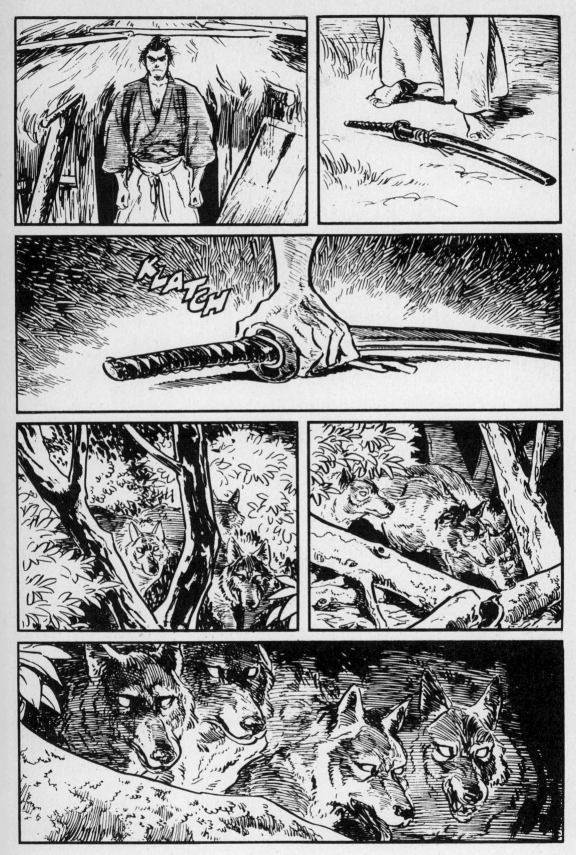

14

15

18

SWISH!

KAEHOK!

23

A PROCESSION BEARS THE HIGH PRIEST *JIKEI-WAJO.*

YOUR *HOLINESS*, WE CAN NOT *DISREGARD* THE *LAW*--EVEN FOR YOU. PERHAPS WE COULD *REPEAL* SOME *LESSER* TAXES. THAT MIGHT *HELP* THE PEOPLE...

YOUR *EXCELLENCY!* OUR *POVERTY* IS JUST AS IT'S ALWAYS BEEN. THE PEASANTS *SELL* THEIR *DAUGHTERS,* ABORT THEIR BABIES, AND SUFFER FROM *HUNGER.* THESE PEOPLE ARE THE *NATION!* THE *SAMURAI* ARE *PARASITES* ON THE BACKS OF THE PEASANTS. *RECONSIDER!*

BUT YOUR HOLINESS! OUR *HAN'S** POVERTY IS WELL KNOWN! WE STILL *OWE* THE RICE MERCHANTS FOR LAST YEAR! WE ARE DOING ALL WE CAN.

I *ASSURE* YOU THE PEASANTS UNDERSTAND YOUR SITUATION. THAT'S WHY EVEN IN THE MIDST OF THIS *FAMINE* THERE HAS BEEN NO *REBELLION*-- AS IN OTHER HANS. MY FIRST PRIORITY IS TO THE PEASANTS. THEY CAN'T JUST *SLAVE* AWAY, WAITING TO *DIE!*

26

*HAN-PROVINCE OR STATE.

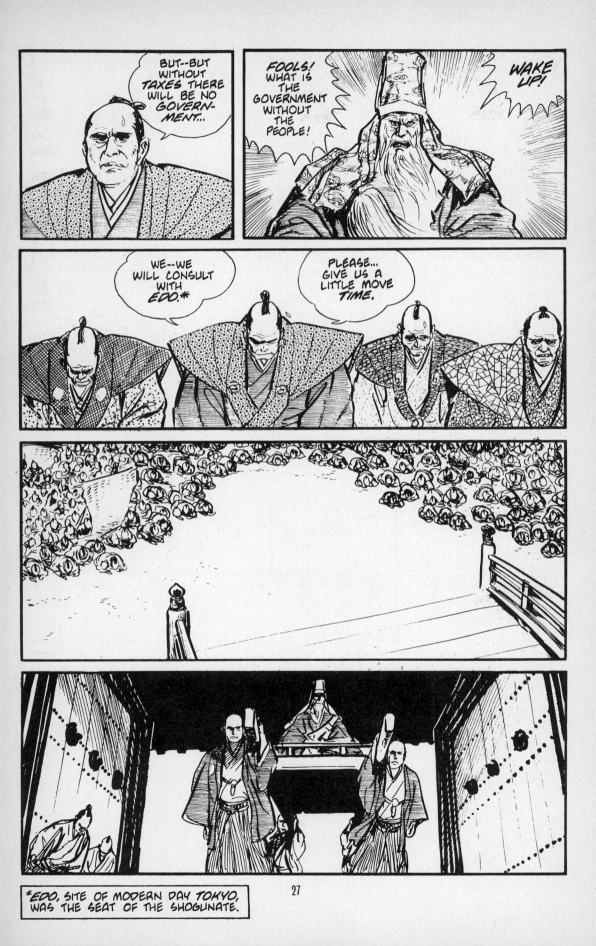

*EDO, SITE OF MODERN DAY TOKYO, WAS THE SEAT OF THE SHOGUNATE.

THE PEASANTS *REVERE JIKEI-WAJO* AS A *LIVING BUDDHA.* OUR LORD *HIROTADA* RESPECTS HIM DEEPLY.

THERE ARE *TWO* PREDOMINATING *FORCES* IN *WAKAGI HAN.* ONE IS *POVERTY,* THE OTHER IS THE *HIGH PRIEST* JIKEI-WAJO OF WAKAGI-GŌTOKUJI TEMPLE.

IT IS BECAUSE OF WAJO THAT WE'VE HAD NO REBELLION DURING THIS FAMINE. WE ALL REALIZE THIS, YET...

HERE, HAVE SOME TEA...

DON'T BOTHER.

I AM AN *ASSASSIN.* JUST GIVE ME THE *FACTS.*

POLITICS ARE JUST *POLITICS--* WE DON'T *PREACH* THE WAY OF BUDDHA.

IF WE DID AS WAJO BID US, THE PEASANTS WOULD GET A *BREAK.*

BUT IF WE DON'T PAY OUR *DEBT* TO THE RICE MERCHANTS, OUR HAN WILL BE *BANKRUPT.*

WE WILL BE THE *LAUGHING* STOCK OF THE COUNTRY...

INDEED, THE COUNTRY WOULD *DIE* WITHOUT THE PEASANTS...

BUT A SAMURAI'S *HONOR* IS GREATER THAN DEATH.

ACCORDING TO WAJO, WE SAMURAI SHOULD *ABANDON* OUR HONOR FOR THE PEASANT'S SAKE.

BUT THIS IS THE WAY OF *BUDDHA,* NOT GOVERNMENT.

SO WHAT YOU WANT IS...

...TO *KILL* THE BUDDHA.

WELL, I CAN'T BELIEVE I HEARD THAT FROM THE FAMOUS *LONE WOLF.* IT IS SAID THAT IN THIS WORLD OF SIX PATHS AND FOUR BIRTHS, THERE IS *NO MAN WHO CAN SLAY A BUDDHA.*

OF COURSE, *HYPOTHETICALLY,* IT MIGHT BE POSSIBLE TO KILL SOMEONE MERELY *POSING* AS A BUDDHA.

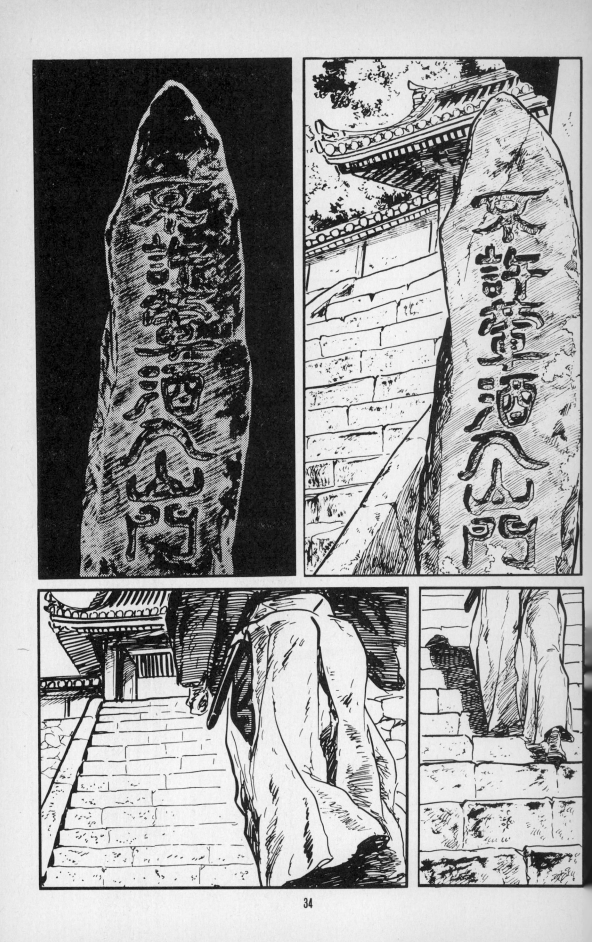

36

TO KILL A MAN, YOU MUST FIRST PROJECT THE *AURA* OF *DEATH*. YOUR OPPONENT *RECIPROCATES*, PROJECTING *HIS* AURA OF DEATH-- OR PERHAPS AN AURA OF *FEAR.* THUS *UNITED* CAN YOU WIELD THE SWORD. THIS IS *MU.*

BUT IF NO AURA *OPPOSES* YOURS... THAT WHICH YOU PROJECT *REBOUNDS* UPON YOU.

IT IS *IMPOSSIBLE* TO MAKE SUCH A CUT. IF YOU *FORCE* YOURSELF, YOU *YOURSELF* WILL BE CUT.

THEN I'VE *FAILED...*

YOU HAVE NOT FAILED. BUT IF YOU CANNOT ACHIEVE *MU* YOU CANNOT *PROCEED.*

YOU CANNOT KILL.

I WHO LIVE IN HELL, PERFORM *HARAKIRI* BEFORE THE BUDDHA.

IF I *CAN'T KILL* YOU, WAJO, I CANNOT LEAD THE *LIFE* OF AN *ASSASSIN*.

THEN *ABANDON* THE ASSASSIN'S ROAD!

I WISH I COULD. YET TO *SURVIVE* I MUST NOT STOP.

THEN IF YOU CAN'T GIVE IT UP YOU MUST ACHIEVE *MUMONKAN*, THE GATELESS BARRIER.

THE *GATELESS BARRIER* ...?

41

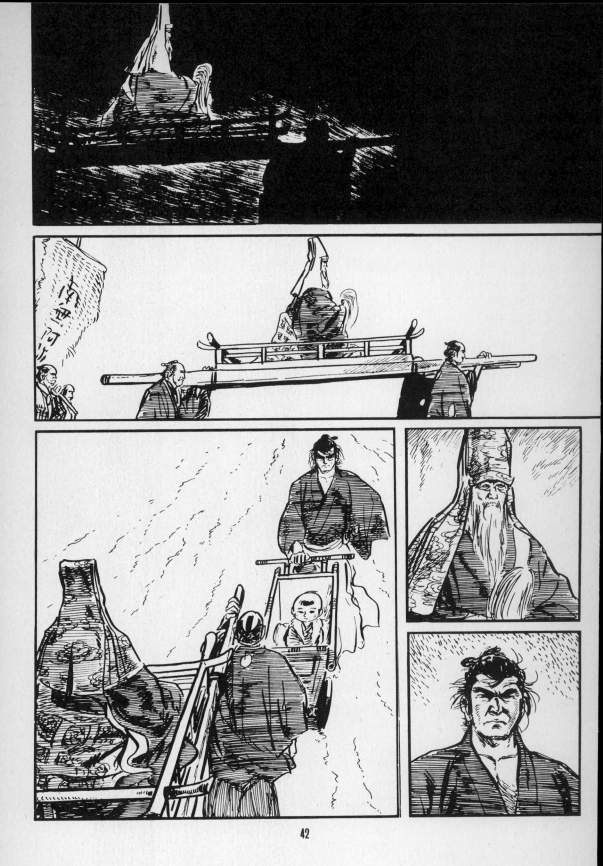

WHOOSH!

44

WAJO-
SAMA!

Y'AAAA!

YOUR
HOLINESS!

48

50

52

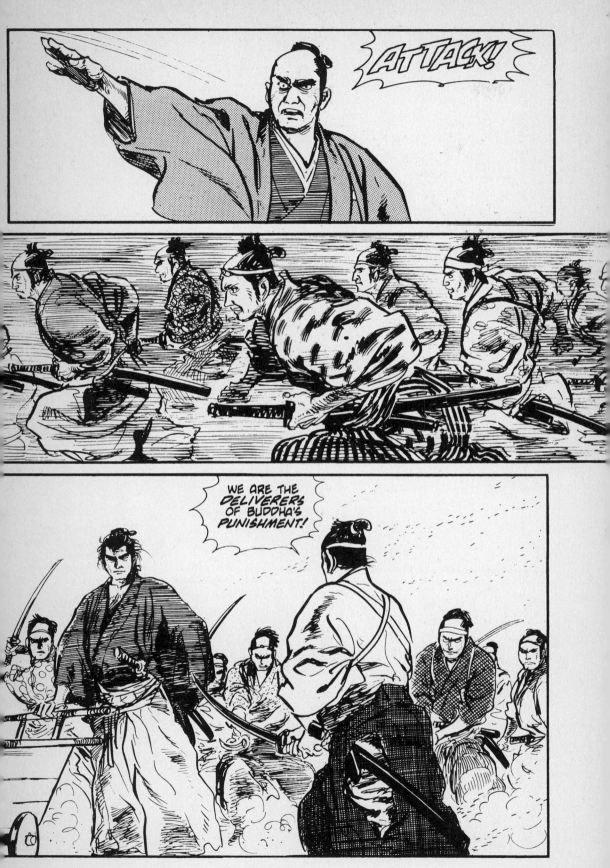

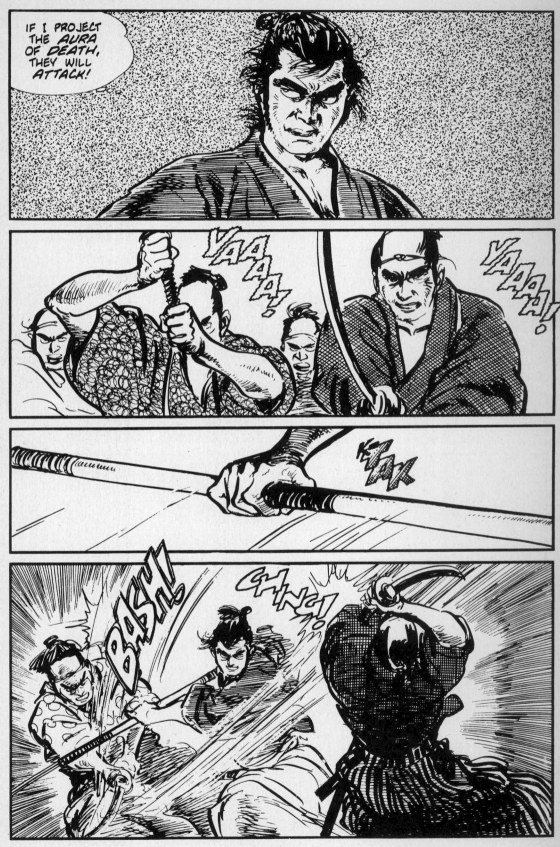

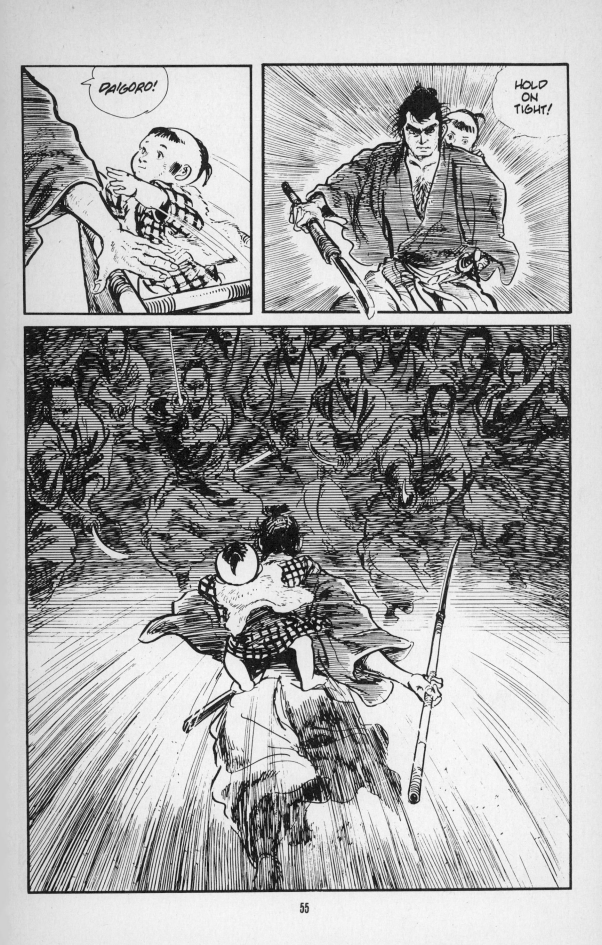

MEET THE BUDDHA,
KILL THE BUDDHA.

59

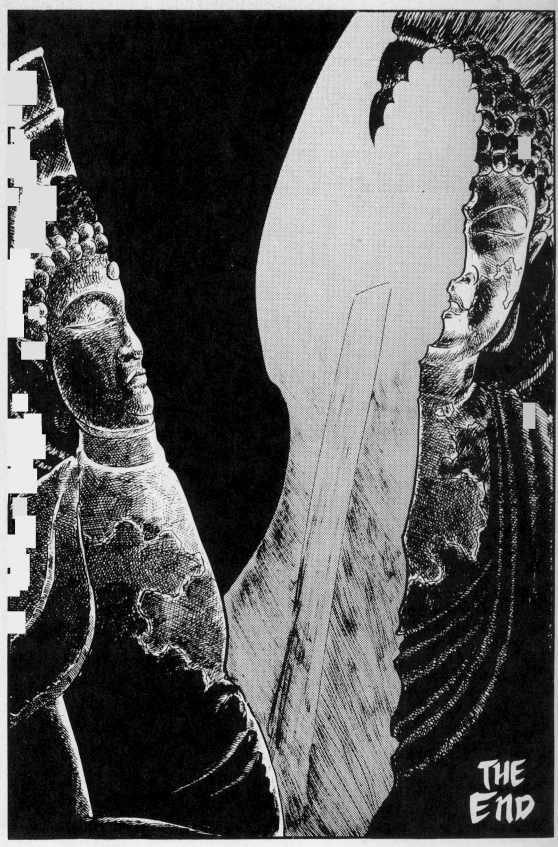

THE END